P9-DFV-034

Word List

Here is a list of words that might make it easier to read this book. You'll find them in boldface the first time they appear in the story.

ballet	BA-lay
studio	STOO-dee-oh
leotard	LEE-uh-tard
barre	bar
ballerina	ba-luh-REE-nah
demi-pointe	duh-mee-PWANT
tendu	tahn-DOO
national	NA-shuh-nuhl
professional	pruh-FE-shuh-nul
tutus	TOO-toos
plié	plee-AY
arabesque	ar-uh-BESK
audition	aw-DI-shuhn
pirouetted	pir-uh-WET-tid
bouquet	boh-KAY
choreographer	kor-ee-AH-gruh-fer
taffeta	TA-fuh-tuh
scenery	SEE-nuh-ree
orchestra	OR-kuhs-truh
applause	uh-PLAWZ

Barbie™

A Special Ballerina

BARBIE and associated trademarks are owned by and used under
license from Mattel, Inc. © 1998 Mattel, Inc. All Rights Reserved.
Published by Grolier Books, a division of Grolier Enterprises, Inc.
Story by Linda Williams Aber and Della Foster. Photo crew: Scott Fujikawa,
Cristina La Bianca, Lars Auvinen, Vince Okada, Susan Cracraft and Judy Tsuno.
Produced by Bumpy Slide Books.
Printed in the United States of America.

ISBN: 0-7172-8831-5

GROLIER
B O O K S

Chapter One

"Hurry along, girls!" Miss Reed called from the **ballet studio.** "Class is starting!"

The dressing room was crowded. Janet, Whitney, and Erin giggled and chattered as they changed out of their school clothes.

"Come on, Katie!" Janet said. "Do you want us to wait for you?"

"No," Katie answered, "that's okay. You guys go ahead." Katie waited until the other girls left. As usual, she was the last one to put on her **leotard.** She pulled her long, brown hair up into a topknot so the teacher could make sure she held

1

her neck and shoulders correctly.

Then with her hair up, Katie left to take her place at the end of the **barre.** She liked this spot best. The mirror didn't go all the way to the other wall. Standing there, Katie couldn't see herself in the mirror.

Katie liked all of the barre exercises. In fact, she liked everything about ballet except the changing-clothes part. It didn't seem fair. Why had all the other girls lost their baby fat when she had so much left? Nobody else seemed to notice it much, except for Nicky, the horrible new boy at school who called her "King Kong Katie." More than anything, Katie wanted to be a **ballerina.** But she was sure as long as the baby fat was there, she could never be a good dancer.

"You'll see," her mother had told her again and again. "It will be gone soon."

But as far as Katie was concerned, "soon" wasn't soon enough.

"First position! Second position! Third position!" Miss Reed called out. **"Demi-pointe! Tendu**!"

Katie loved the sound of the French words. She knew that all the names of the steps were in French because the first **national** ballet school had been in France. That was something all good ballet students knew.

Slowly the teacher walked along the line of students. She stopped in front of each girl and moved a foot or a hand into the correct position. As usual, when she came to Katie, Miss Reed didn't change a thing. "Perfect!" she said proudly.

Katie smiled. Then she saw Barbie watching her from the doorway. Barbie gave her a thumbs-up and winked. "Good job, Katie!" she whispered.

The smile on Katie's face grew bigger. She was glad to see Barbie. Katie had been best friends with Barbie's sister Stacie for as long as she could remember. Barbie had even been Katie's baby-sitter.

3

Now Barbie had a full-time job as a **professional** ballet dancer for the City Ballet Company.

In fact, Katie was excited for another reason. The next day, Barbie would be taking Katie and Stacie to the City Ballet Theater for a backstage tour. Then they would watch Barbie dance in the afternoon show. Katie couldn't wait to see what went on behind the scenes at a real ballet performance!

Katie watched Barbie in the mirror and saw her go into another practice room. She knew Barbie would spend hours there. Being a real ballet dancer wasn't easy. Barbie went to the City Ballet Theater to practice with the other dancers every day. She started early in the morning and took a short break for lunch. After the group practice was finished, she went to Miss Reed's studio and practiced some more on her own.

Barbie told Katie that at night she took long baths to soak her sore muscles. Bedtime for Barbie was early so she could get up the next day and go to the theater to practice again. Barbie always said, "Ballet is more than just toe shoes and **tutus.** Ballet is hard work!"

"Stretches now, girls!" Miss Reed called over the music. "Bend! Arms out! **Plié! Arabesque!** Bend and stop!"

Barbie was right. Ballet was hard work. When the class was over, Miss Reed clapped her hands and the music stopped. All the girls stood up straight at the barre.

"I have something very exciting to tell you," Miss Reed said. "In two weeks, the City Ballet Company will have tryouts for *The Nutcracker.* This is the first year that you girls are old enough to **audition.** One girl from this class will be chosen. I hope you will all try out."

All the girls jumped up and down with excitement. As they hurried to the dressing room, everyone talked about the tryouts.

"Wow!" exclaimed Janet. "Who do you think

they'll pick, Katie?"

Katie just shrugged her shoulders. While the other girls talked and changed their clothes, Katie pretended to be looking for something in her ballet bag. When everyone had left, she stood in front of the mirror and looked at herself. She turned sideways and tried to suck in her tummy. It was no use. It wouldn't get smaller.

Of course, nobody really knew who would be chosen to perform in *The Nutcracker.* But Katie was sure she wouldn't be picked. She changed back into her skirt and sweater. Picking up her ballet bag, she headed for the door. She hoped her mother would be late picking her up. She wanted to stay and watch Barbie practice. Luckily, when Katie poked her head out the door, her mom wasn't there yet.

Katie walked to the studio where Barbie was hard at work. Barbie's blond hair was pulled up into a tight bun. She wore a purple practice leotard and pink toe shoes. Katie watched as Barbie **pirouetted,** making turn after turn across the floor. She looked confident. Barbie held her head high. She had practiced this routine many, many times.

Katie wasn't thinking about her tummy or the tryouts now. She was only thinking how proud she was to know Barbie, a real professional ballerina. She hoped that someday she would be one, too.

Chapter Two

Katie woke up to the smell of pancakes and maple syrup. It was Saturday morning, and Saturday breakfasts at her house were always special. But this day was even more special. This was the day she and Stacie were going to take the backstage tour and see Barbie dance!

"Katie!" her mother called up the stairs. "Hey, sleepyhead! Dad's already been to the store and back. Are you up yet?"

"Almost!" Katie answered, crawling out of bed. As her feet touched the floor, she did a ballet twirl across her room. She landed in front of the full-length mirror on her closet door. Katie took a bow and held out her arms to take a pretend **bouquet** of flowers from an imaginary audience. "Thank you!" she said into the mirror. "Thank you all!"

Katie laughed at herself. She was pretending to be a famous ballet dancer again. In her flowing nightgown, she always felt like a ballerina princess. "Why can't ballerinas wear nightgowns instead of leotards?" she wondered. Then she wouldn't have to worry about a little tummy trouble.

Katie dressed in her nicest outfit and bounced down the stairs and into the kitchen. In the middle of her plate stood a neat stack of three pancakes. She stabbed two with her fork and dropped them onto her mother's plate.

"Oh, no," her mother said quickly. "No pancakes for me, thanks. Would you like to share some of my melon instead, honey?"

Even though Katie knew she'd be hungry

later, she replied, "No thanks, Mom. This is fine."

As Katie swallowed the last bit of breakfast, a car horn honked outside. She ran to the door and looked out. Barbie's car had just pulled up in front of the house.

"Hi, Stacie! Hi, Barbie!" Katie called out. "Bye, mom!"

Barbie smiled and waved. Stacie was already out of the car and holding the door open for Katie.

"Your car, Madam," Stacie said with a laugh.

"Hi, Katie!" Barbie said cheerfully. "Are you ready for a day at the ballet?"

"Oh, yes!" Katie replied. "I can't wait to see you dance, Barbie!"

It was a short ride to the theater. Soon Barbie, Katie, and Stacie stood in front of a big, black door. The words STAGE DOOR were printed on it in white letters. This door was special. It was only for people who worked at the City Ballet Theater. As Barbie turned the doorknob, Katie squealed with excitement. "I can't believe how lucky we are!" she said.

"Shhh!" Barbie whispered. "We have to be very quiet. The **choreographer** is going over some of the dance steps with a few new dancers. The choreographer creates and arranges all the dances in the ballet."

Barbie held the heavy stage door open for Katie and Stacie. Sounds of violins and a piano filled the dimly lit hallway. The music was coming from somewhere above.

"The stage is upstairs," Barbie explained. "The dressing and practice rooms are down here."

Barbie led the way. Stacie and Katie followed closely behind.

"Look at all these beautiful dresses," Katie whispered to Stacie.

Katie was pointing to racks and racks of colorful costumes. On one rack she saw velvet gowns and beaded capes. Dozens of shimmering

silver leotards and skirts hung neatly on another rack. One more rack was filled with pink, white, and blue **taffeta** skirts.

"We keep the people who design and sew costumes very busy," Barbie explained. "The costume designers read the ballet script and character descriptions. Then they make drawings of each costume. When the designs are final, the seamstresses begin sewing."

"That must take days!" Stacie gasped.

"More like weeks or months," said Barbie. "Each scene of the ballet has a different set of costumes. When the dancers come offstage, we need to be able to find the next costumes easily. So each rack has a different scene's costumes."

Barbie kept walking. She pointed out the different dressing rooms along the way. When they came to a door with a star on it, Barbie opened it. She turned on a light. Katie and Stacie could not believe their eyes. There were flowers everywhere from Barbie's fans! Beautiful costumes were hanging on a rack against one wall. A mirror framed in lights hung over a makeup table. The table was covered with jars, bottles, and tubes of stage makeup.

"Well," Barbie laughed, "now you see how messy a dressing room can be!"

A man with twinkling blue eyes and a neat white beard knocked on the open door. "One hour until show time, Barbie," he said cheerfully. Then he went down the row of doors in the hallway. He knocked on each door. "One hour until show time," he said again and again in his merry voice.

"That's Mr. Glover," Barbie explained. "He's our stage manager. He keeps everything in order in the dressing room area. He also makes sure the costumes are where we can find them. And when it's time for the show to begin, he's the messenger between the director and the performers. He lets us know in plenty of time when we should start

15

getting ready to go onstage."

Katie and Stacie listened to every word. Both of them thought that what went on backstage was every bit as interesting as what happened onstage.

When the man came back, Barbie called him into the dressing room. "Mr. Glover," she said, "this is my sister Stacie and her friend Katie. They are my guests today. I've saved two seats for them. Would you please show them where to sit while I get ready?" She handed Mr. Glover two tickets.

"Sure, Barbie," he replied. "Right this way, young ladies!"

Barbie gave each of the girls a big hug. "I'll be watching you!" she said, winking at them both.

"We'll be watching you, too!" Katie laughed.

Chapter Three

After saying good-bye to Barbie, the two girls followed Mr. Glover up a flight of stairs. On the way, he pointed out more interesting things behind the scenes. "Here, girls," he said, touching a giant toy soldier made out of wood, "this fellow is part of one of the sets. He'll be wheeled onto the stage when he's needed."

"Did you make the sets?" Stacie asked. "I think making the sets is the best job of all."

Mr. Glover laughed. "No, I don't make the sets. I leave the artwork to the set designers and **scenery** painters."

17

Stacie stopped to examine the soldier and some other plywood figures. "They all look so huge!" she said.

"That's so even the people sitting in the balcony section can see them," Mr. Glover explained. "Everything that's on the stage has to be very large so people sitting far away can see it."

"Is that why the dancers wear so much makeup?" Stacie asked.

"Exactly!" Mr. Glover answered. "The makeup artists know just how much to use so the dancer's features can be seen from far away."

"Wow!" Katie exclaimed. "Choreographers, set designers, costume designers, makeup artists. I never knew it took so many people to put on a show!"

"That's right, Katie. And you and Stacie are about to become one of the most important parts of the show!" said Mr. Glover.

"We are?" Stacie and Katie asked together.

"Of course. You're part of the audience!" Mr. Glover said cheerfully. "We can't have a show without an audience!" He pushed open a big red door and let Katie and Stacie go through first.

"Oh!" Katie gasped. "I never thought of it that way."

The audience was already filing in and sitting down. Mr. Glover showed the girls to their seats in the center of the first row. "Enjoy the show!" he said.

Katie and Stacie thanked the kind man and said good-bye. Shortly after they settled into their seats, the lights in the theater began to dim. Soon the **orchestra** began to play. The velvet curtain rose. The spotlight came on. And there was Barbie, looking more beautiful than Katie had ever seen her look before.

"That's how I want to look," Katie said to herself. Katie couldn't take her eyes off Barbie.

She seemed to float across the stage. Every movement Barbie made was graceful. Every step she took was steady and sure. All of Barbie's hours of practice showed in her performance.

The time went by too quickly for Katie. When the ballet performers took their final bow, Barbie stepped forward for one last curtsy. The **applause** sounded like thunder to Katie. But her own clapping was the loudest of all.

Slowly the audience left the theater. Stacie and Katie sat back down and waited for Barbie to come and get them.

When everyone was gone, the girls heard Barbie calling them. "Katie! Stacie!" she shouted. "Up here!"

The girls looked up at the stage. There was Barbie, still wearing her costume. "Come up here!" she told them. "Come see how it feels to be a real ballerina."

Katie and Stacie rushed up the stairs on one

side of the stage. Right away Stacie walked to the back of the stage and began exploring the sets. But Katie walked to center stage and took third position, with her feet turned out, one heel behind the other. She looked out at the empty seats.

Barbie called out, "Hey, Joe, hit the spot!"

Suddenly a spotlight came on, and Katie was caught in the light.

"You're the star now, Katie!" Barbie said.

Stacie and Barbie clapped for Katie. For a few seconds, Katie really felt like a star. But the feeling went away when she looked down and saw her own shadow. It wasn't the tall, thin shadow she thought a star ballerina should have. "I'm not a star," she said softly to herself. "I'm only me."

Chapter Four

At school on Monday, Stacie spotted Katie in the cafeteria. "Over here, Katie!" Stacie called from the table across the room. "We saved you a seat!"

Katie smiled and gave a big wave to Stacie. She carried her lunch tray over to the table where Stacie, Erin, Whitney, and Janet sat. Everybody called this the "Ballet and Company Table." The ballet-class girls and Stacie always ate together.

Today they were all talking at once about *The Nutcracker.* Even though Stacie wasn't a dancer, she was very excited for her friends about the tryouts coming up. "I just know you'll make it!" she said to Katie.

"But don't you think we all have a chance?" Janet asked.

"Well, Miss Reed is a really good teacher," Erin said, taking a sip of milk. "If she thinks we should all try out, she must think we all have a chance of making it."

"But Stacie's right," Whitney said. "Katie probably has the best chance."

Katie smiled and looked down at her tray. "Thanks," she said shyly.

Suddenly Stacie stood up and raised her right hand. "We have to promise right now," she said seriously, "that no matter what happens we'll all stay friends."

"Of course we will," Katie began. "I just hope—"

But before Katie could finish her sentence, a hand reached over her shoulder and grabbed the package of chocolate chip cookies off her tray. It was Nicky, the pesty new boy who seemed to spend all his free time teasing the girls.

"Hey, Nicky!" Stacie shouted. "Give those cookies back to Katie!"

"King Kong Katie doesn't need cookies!" the boy laughed. "She looks like she's had more than enough to eat already!"

Stacie leaned over and tried to grab the cookies from Nicky. But he was too quick and ran off.

Katie was trying hard not to cry.

"Forget about Nicky," Stacie said to Katie. "Sticks and stones may break your bones, but names will never hurt you!"

Katie smiled just a little bit. She knew that old saying. But it wasn't true. Names *did* hurt her, especially names like "King Kong Katie." Katie knew what Nicky was really saying. "He's saying I'm fat!" she thought.

The talk at the table turned back to *The*

Nutcracker. While the other girls made plans to get together for practices, Katie was quiet.

"You're going to practice with us, aren't you, Katie?" Janet asked.

Katie wasn't thinking about practice or the tryouts. She was thinking about Nicky and what he had said.

For the rest of the lunch hour Katie didn't say much. Stacie tried to cheer her up. She even shared her chocolate chip cookies with Katie. But for some reason, the cookies didn't really taste that good to Katie.

Chapter Five

"T.G.I.F.!" Janet was saying to Erin just as Katie stepped into the dressing room at the dance studio. "Thank Goodness It's Friday!"

"You can say that again!" Erin agreed.

"Thank Goodness It's Friday!" Janet said again.

All the girls laughed. Katie had to laugh, too. In fact, she hadn't laughed much since Monday. The teasing from Nicky was still bothering her. She had been thinking about it all week. Nothing Stacie said made her feel any better. And whenever anyone even said the word *big,* Katie was sure they were talking about her waistline.

By the middle of the week, Katie had decided she was not going to try out for *The Nutcracker.* She hadn't told anyone yet. But she had made up her mind, even though she felt sad about it.

Now that it was Friday and time for ballet class, Katie had built up the courage to tell Miss Reed that she wasn't going to try out. But before she had a chance to talk to her, the teacher surprised the girls with an announcement.

"Good afternoon, girls!" Miss Reed said, peeking into the dressing room.

"Good afternoon, Miss Reed," the class replied politely.

"Girls," Miss Reed continued, "I have an important meeting to attend with the directors of the City Ballet Company to talk about the tryouts. So I won't be teaching your class today. But I think you'll be happy to hear that Barbie will be taking my place as your teacher today!"

"Barbie!" Katie shouted, feeling happier than she'd felt all week. "That's great!"

Miss Reed smiled. "I thought you'd be pleased. But don't think it's going to be an easy class today. The tryouts are next week. I know you all want to be ready. Hurry now and get changed. Barbie is waiting."

"But Miss Reed," Katie began.

"Not now, Katie," the teacher said kindly. "I have to hurry to my meeting, and you have to hurry to class."

"Yes, Miss Reed," Katie said softly.

The teacher waved good-bye and left the girls to finish getting ready. Because Barbie was their teacher, even Katie changed her clothes a little faster than usual. She didn't wait for the others to leave. Instead, she quickly put on her leotard and hurried into the ballet studio with the rest of the group.

Barbie stood up straight. "Hi, girls!" she

greeted the class cheerfully. "Take your places at the barre. We'll do some warm-ups first."

The girls lined up at the barre. Katie took her usual place. For once she wished the mirror went all the way to the end of the barre. She wanted to be able to see Barbie and follow her motions exactly. Before she could move down just a bit, the warm-up music began.

Barbie stood in first position, her feet turned out, heels and calves touching. "All right, girls," she called out. "One and bend! Two and bend! Three and bend! Keep your hands firmly on the barre. Eyes to the mirror. Shoulders straight. Don't tighten your knees. Relax and bend!"

Barbie worked with them on arm movements and hand positions. "Each of you should think of yourself as a graceful snowflake," she said. "You're not dancing. You're gently floating through the air."

Katie worked even harder than usual. Her arms gracefully moved up and down, back and forth. Her hands felt lighter than air as she turned her wrists in and out.

"That's it, Katie!" Barbie said, smiling. "Girls," she said to the others, "watch how Katie's arms seem to float."

The class watched Katie and tried to follow the same motions with their arms and hands.

"Very good!" Barbie said to each of them. "Excellent! You're all floating now!"

The hour flew by. When the class was over, the girls thanked Barbie and hurried to the changing room. Barbie put a hand out to stop Katie. She wanted to talk with her. "Can you stay after class for a few minutes?" she asked Katie. "It's important."

"Sure, I guess so," Katie said a little nervously. "Did I do something wrong?"

Barbie laughed. "Oh, no, Katie. You didn't do anything wrong. In fact, you did everything right! That's why I want to spend some extra time

with you. I think you are very talented."

Katie couldn't believe what she was hearing! On Monday, Nicky had called her "King Kong Katie." Now, on Friday, Barbie was calling her "talented."

"Talented?" Katie asked slowly. "Me?"

"Yes, you," Barbie said. "I was watching you very carefully during the class. With a little extra work, you'll have an excellent chance of getting a part in *The Nutcracker.* I'd love to work with you to get you ready."

"Oh, thank you!" Katie said, blushing a bright red. "But I'm not trying out."

"Not trying out!" Barbie exclaimed. "But why not?"

Katie looked down at her feet for a few seconds. "I guess I'm just not that interested. I mean I'm so busy. You know, homework and chores for my mom take up a lot of time."

"Yes," Barbie said, "homework and chores

are important. But I'm guessing that you think dancing is important, too. We all have to make time for the things that matter most to us. Do you remember how good you felt when you were standing on the stage at the City Ballet Theater?"

"Yes," Katie said, "I remember."

"Just think about it," Barbie said, patting Katie on the shoulder. "Think about it and let me know if you change your mind. And remember what I told you today. You have real talent."

On the car ride home with her dad, Katie was quiet. She was thinking about everything that Barbie had said. She remembered how good it felt to stand in the spotlight on a real stage. She would rather be a dancer like Barbie than be anything else. But she also couldn't forget how it felt to be called "King Kong Katie." After that, the last thing Katie wanted was to have an audience full of people looking at her. Standing in a spotlight was the last place she wanted to be.

Chapter Six

When Katie got home from ballet class, her mom was on the phone. She waved hello to Katie but kept talking in a serious voice.

Katie carried her ballet bag up to her room. Closing the door behind her, she dropped the bag onto the floor and flopped down on the bed. She looked up at the wall over her bed. On it were framed photos of famous ballerinas. They all looked perfect in their tutus and pink satin toe shoes. But her favorite pictures were the ones she had taped up by herself. They showed dancers working hard at practice. They were fixing their shoes, or stretching and straining at the barre. Those dancers always reminded her of what she liked best about dancing.

Katie stared at the pictures for a while. She imagined she was one of those dancers in the photos. Suddenly her stomach growled to remind her she had skipped her lunch.

"Oh, be quiet, stomach!" Katie said to herself. She reached into a drawer and pulled out a piece of chewing gum. She folded the stick of gum in half and popped it into her mouth. "There!" she said to her stomach. "Now are you happy?"

Her stomach had been growling a lot since Nicky hurt her feelings on Monday. She had been trying to eat less. She hoped it would make her look like the other girls who had already lost their baby fat. She even hoped if she ate less it would make her a better dancer.

"Maybe it's working," she said to herself. "After all, Barbie said I was a good dancer."

Katie chewed the gum and hoped it would make her feel full. To take her mind off food, she stuck a tape into her tape player. It was the music from ballet class.

Katie kicked off her sneakers. She dug around in her bag and pulled out her practice ballet slippers. Soon her thoughts were about the things Barbie had taught in class. She moved her arms back and forth, up and down. She turned and bent down gracefully to touch the floor with her fingertips. Her feet and hands followed the music perfectly.

When the music came to Katie's favorite part, she tried a new position. With one foot on the floor and an arm in the air for balance, she lifted her other arm and leg behind her. Then she twisted her head over her shoulder and couldn't believe her eyes. Barbie was standing in her doorway!

"Barbie!" Katie said, turning around. "What

are you doing here?"

Barbie laughed. "I guess you didn't hear me knocking on the door. You were too busy practicing."

Katie smoothed her hair and turned off the tape player. "I was just going over some of the things you taught us in class today," she explained.

"I thought you were too busy for this," said Barbie, smiling. "You know, all that homework . . . and chores for your mom."

"Well . . ." Katie began.

Barbie put an arm around Katie's shoulder. "Sit down with me for a minute," she said. "It seems like there's more than just homework and chores on your mind. Stacie told me what happened in the lunchroom on Monday. And your mom and I had a talk on the phone today. She told me how proud she is of you and your dancing."

Tears filled Katie's eyes. All week she had been holding them back. Now she couldn't stop them. As the tears came out, so did her story. Katie told Barbie everything. She told her about the dressing room at ballet class. She told her about taking her place at the end of the barre just to hide from the mirror. And finally Katie told Barbie how hard she had been trying to eat less so she would look like everyone else in the class.

Barbie gave Katie a big hug. Then she pulled out a tissue and wiped Katie's tears away. "Katie," she said gently, "it seems to me that Nicky is not your biggest problem."

"He's not?" Katie said, wiping a tear from her cheek. "Then what is?"

"You," Barbie explained. "Try not to worry about what Nicky says or thinks about you. Learn to like yourself a little better instead."

"I like myself," Katie said. "I just don't like my tummy!"

Barbie laughed. But then she talked seriously to Katie for a long time. She told Katie how important it was to realize that everyone is different and special in his or her own way. She said it was silly to try to be anyone but yourself. "Remember the snowflakes in practice today?" Barbie asked. "Well, people are a lot like snowflakes. No two are exactly alike. But each snowflake is beautiful and special, right?"

Katie nodded.

"You are a one-of-a-kind person, Katie," said Barbie. "You don't need to try to be like anyone else. You've worked very hard to become a good dancer. How you look has nothing to do with how you dance, or who you are inside."

Katie sighed and felt the tears coming again.

Barbie hugged her. "Everybody else likes you because of who you are, Katie. Now it's time for you to start liking yourself. And when you like yourself, you will want to take good care of yourself," Barbie explained. "That means getting plenty of sleep, exercising, and eating right. To be good dancers, we need to be strong. To be strong, we need to be healthy, and that comes from treating our bodies right."

"Really?" asked Katie.

"Yes," replied Barbie. She stood up to leave, but turned to say one more thing. "Be yourself, Katie. You are a very, very special young lady."

"And that's why you think I should try out?" asked Katie.

"Definitely!" answered Barbie. "Your talent in ballet should be expressed, not hidden. I hope you'll think about what I've said."

"I will. Thanks, Barbie," Katie said as she walked Barbie to the door.

When Barbie left, Katie sat down on her bed. She tried to think of what there was to like about herself. She took out a piece of paper and a pen from her desk drawer and made two lists:

Things I Will Do to Take Care of Myself

    1. Eat right.

    2. Get plenty of sleep.

    3. Exercise.

Things I Like about Myself

    1. I am kind.

    2. I am smart.

    3. I am funny.

    4. I am a good friend.

    5.

When Katie came to number five, she stopped. She thought and she thought. Then her eyes brightened. "I've got it!" Katie said. In big, bold letters, Katie wrote:

5. I AM A GOOD DANCER!

Suddenly Katie knew exactly what she was

going to do. She put on her tape of *The Nutcracker* and listened carefully, reworking her routine over and over in her head.

Then after a good, healthful dinner, Katie went to her room and dialed Barbie's number. She wanted to tell Barbie her decision.

"Hello, Barbie?" she said. "This is Katie. I just wanted to tell you I changed my mind. I'm not too busy to practice ballet with you. And we'd better start soon, because I'm going to try out after all!"

Chapter Seven

"Again, Katie!" Barbie called over the music in the practice studio. "Up, down, up, and turn! Up, down, up, and turn! That's it! You've got it!"

"Bravo!" Stacie shouted from where she sat on a folding chair in the corner. Every day that week, Katie had come to the ballet studio to practice with Barbie. At last the day of the tryouts was here.

Katie felt good. In fact, she felt great. Since her talk with Barbie, she had been following all of Barbie's advice. She'd made sure that she ate a good breakfast every morning. At lunchtime she'd chosen an apple or banana for dessert instead of cookies. And at dinner, she'd made sure to eat the vegetables instead of just pushing them around on her plate.

When bedtime came, Katie had made sure she was in bed on time. She'd been surprised to find herself waking up earlier. She'd even had time to practice for fifteen minutes every morning before she got dressed.

It hadn't taken long for Katie to realize that Barbie was right. Taking good care of herself had made Katie like herself a lot better.

"Bravo!" Stacie shouted again. "Your routine looks great!"

Barbie smiled proudly. "Yes," she agreed, "I think you've worked very hard this week, Katie, and not only on your ballet!"

Katie smiled back at Barbie. But before she could say anything, there was a knock on the door. Miss Reed poked her head in. "Katie," her teacher said, "it's time to join the other girls. Tryouts are about to begin!"

"Oh, Katie!" Stacie said, grabbing Katie's arm excitedly. "I hope you get it!"

"Thanks, Stacie," Katie replied softly. And then, to Barbie, she said, "And thank you, too, for all you've done."

Barbie winked at Katie. "You're the one who has done it, Katie. Now let's hurry! The judges are waiting!"

Stacie, Barbie, and Katie walked down the hall to the performance studio where the tryouts were being held. They walked past a small group of parents who were waiting to go in to watch. Katie waved to her own parents as she hurried past.

To Katie's surprise, and horror, Nicky was there also! "What's he doing here?" she whispered nervously to Stacie.

"His sister is trying out, remember?" Stacie whispered back. "Forget about him."

Stacie switched sides with Katie to block Nicky's view as they walked by him. Then Miss Reed came out to tell the group of parents that they could come into the studio. Katie felt more relaxed about Nicky's being there when she heard Miss Reed say that everyone would have to be quiet during the tryouts. Barbie and Stacie took their seats in the front, next to Miss Reed.

Katie joined the other girls in the front of the room. They waited for their names to be called. The four judges from the City Ballet Company sat at a table facing the stage. They introduced themselves and announced the order in which the girls would try out. Katie would be the last one.

Katie watched as each girl took her turn. She was amazed at how good all the girls were. This was the first time she had ever really watched each of them dance. She had been so busy worrying about how she looked that she hadn't taken the time to notice how her friends were doing in class.

"Maybe no one was really looking at me, either," she thought to herself.

At the end of each girl's performance, the judges wrote down notes and then held up score cards. Katie felt happy for everyone because, so far, they had all done very well.

At last it was Katie's turn. She walked to the center of the stage and stood in position. She looked beyond the heads of the judges. Behind them she could see Barbie and Stacie smiling proudly. The music began to play, and Katie started dancing. She didn't feel nervous or afraid. All her practicing had prepared her for this moment. She didn't have to think of what to do with her arms and feet. Every movement came naturally to her. The music led her through a perfect ballet routine.

Applause filled the room. All the girls who had tried out were clapping wildly for Katie. Barbie, Stacie, and Miss Reed were standing and clapping, too. Katie looked up and saw the judges holding up their score cards. To her surprise, she had received a perfect score from each of them!

"All right!" Stacie exclaimed. "You did it!"

"I did?" Katie said. "I mean, I did! I did!"

Everyone rushed up to Katie. All her friends hugged her and told her how great her performance had been. It made Katie feel good inside to know that her friends were happy for her. And deep down, she was happy, too, whether or not she got the part.

But the biggest surprise of all came when Nicky came up to her. "Uh, Katie," he said shyly, "I, uh, well, er, nice job." Then he blushed and said, "You're an awesome dancer!"

Katie couldn't believe her own ears! Nicky the teaser, Nicky the name-caller, had just told her she was awesome! Maybe now he'd stop calling her names. Maybe he wasn't so bad after all, Katie thought with a smile. "Thanks, Nicky," she replied. "Thanks a lot!"

"Don't mention it," Nicky said. "See you later, okay? Katie, Katie, The Ballet Lady!"

Katie laughed. "Oh, well," she said to Stacie and Barbie as they walked off the stage arm in arm, "at least that's a name I can live with!"